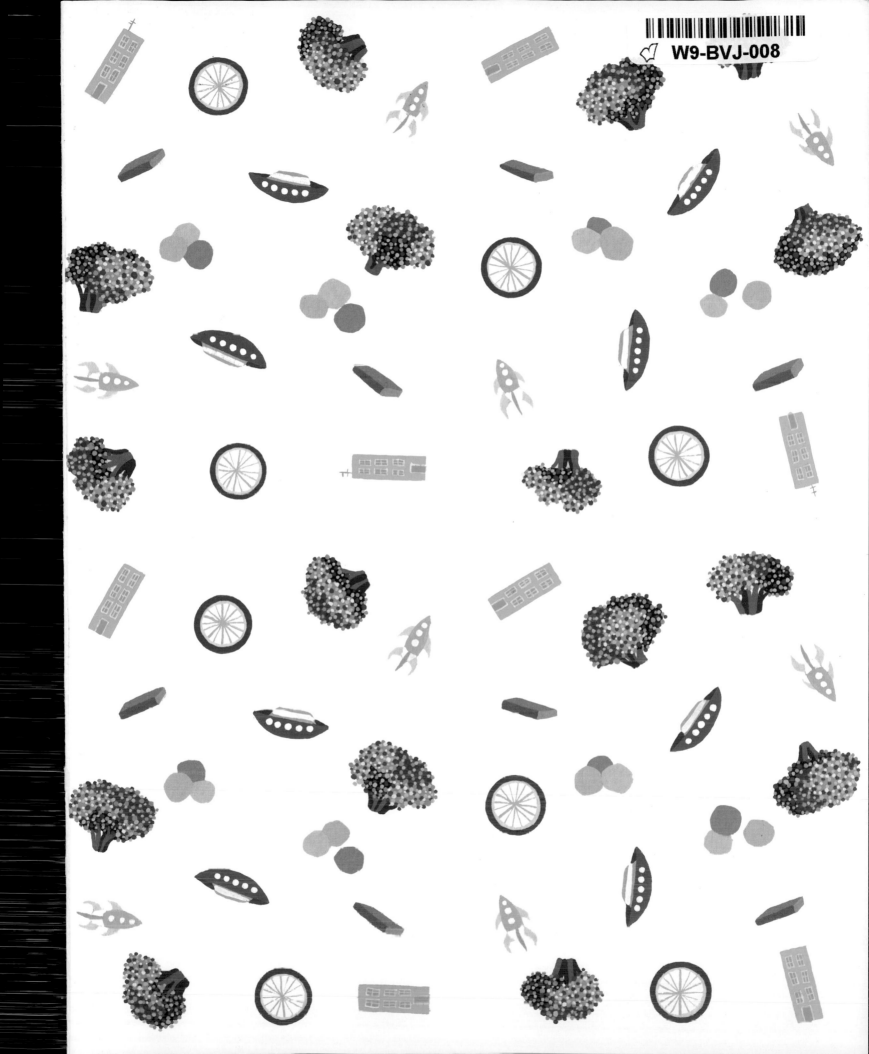

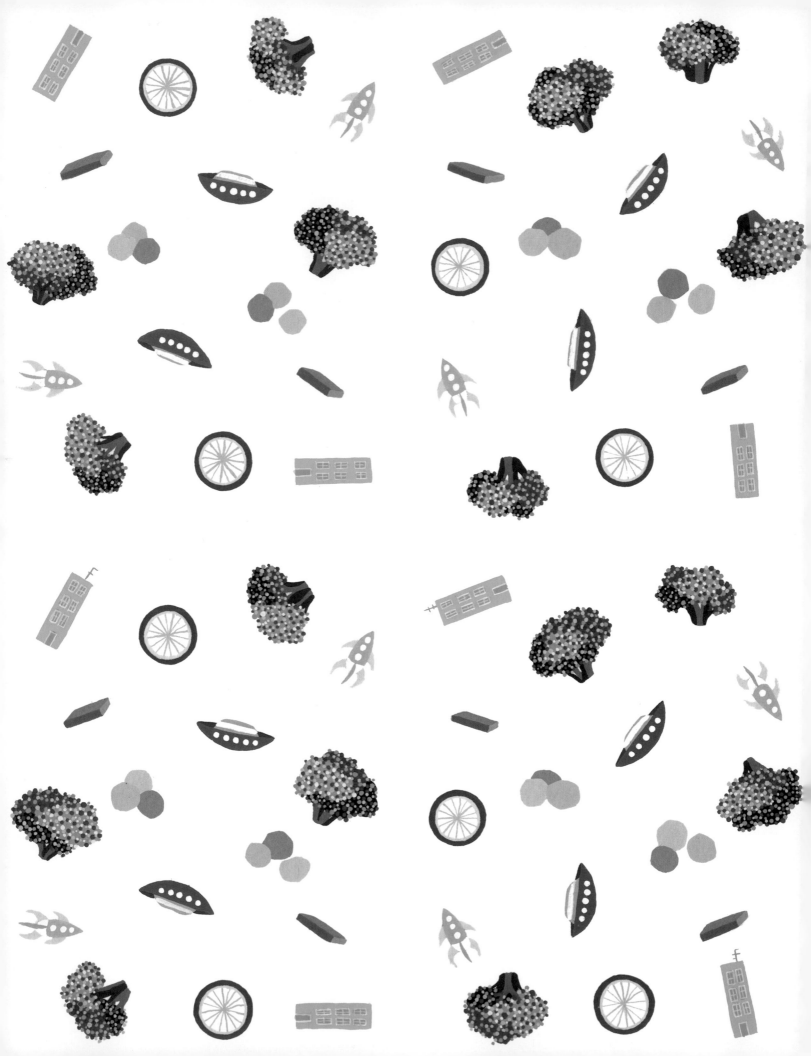

MONSTERs DON'T eat BROCCOLI

For Papa, who loves his veggies!
—B.J.H.

For my lovely boyfriend, Paul
—S.H.

The Library of Congress has cataloged the hardcover edition of this work as follows:
Hicks, Barbara Jean.
Monsters don't eat broccoli / by Barbara Jean Hicks ; illustrated by Sue Hendra. — 1st ed.
p. cm.
Summary: Illustrations and rhyming text reveal how imagination can spice up even the healthiest meal.
ISBN 978-0-375-85686-0 (trade) — ISBN 978-0-375-95686-7 (lib. bdg.)
[1. Stories in rhyme. 2. Monsters—Fiction. 3. Food habits—Fiction.] I. Hendra, Sue, ill. II. Title.
PZ8.3.H5328Mon 2009 [E]—dc22 2008024536

ISBN 978-0-385-75521-4 (trade pbk.)

MANUFACTURED IN CHINA

10 9

First Dragonfly Books Edition

MONSTERS DON'T eat BROCCOLI

By Barbara Jean Hicks

Illustrated by Sue Hendra

Dragonfly Books ⟶ New York

The waitress in this restaurant
just doesn't have a clue.

Monsters don't eat broccoli!
How could she think we do?

We'd rather snack on tractors

or a rocket ship or two,

or tender trailer tidbits,

or a wheely, steely stew.

Monsters don't eat broccoli or artichokes or greens.

We can't abide alfalfa sprouts
or slimy lima beans.

But redwoods are delectable.

And boulders—what a treat!

And a fountain's so refreshing
in this dreadful summer heat.

"Fum, foe, fie, fee,
monsters don't eat broccoli!"

We're crazy for construction,

and we crave our fish 'n' ships—

but monsters don't eat broccoli.
It will not pass our lips.

You cannot force us monsters to eat vegetables we hate.

Let humans have the garden— we will eat the garden gate!

Monsters love a picnic
on a blanket in the park,

with a clump of giant maples
and their yummy, gummy bark. . . .

FRUITY
OIL

"Fum, foe, fie, fee—
You're chowing down

Another helping,

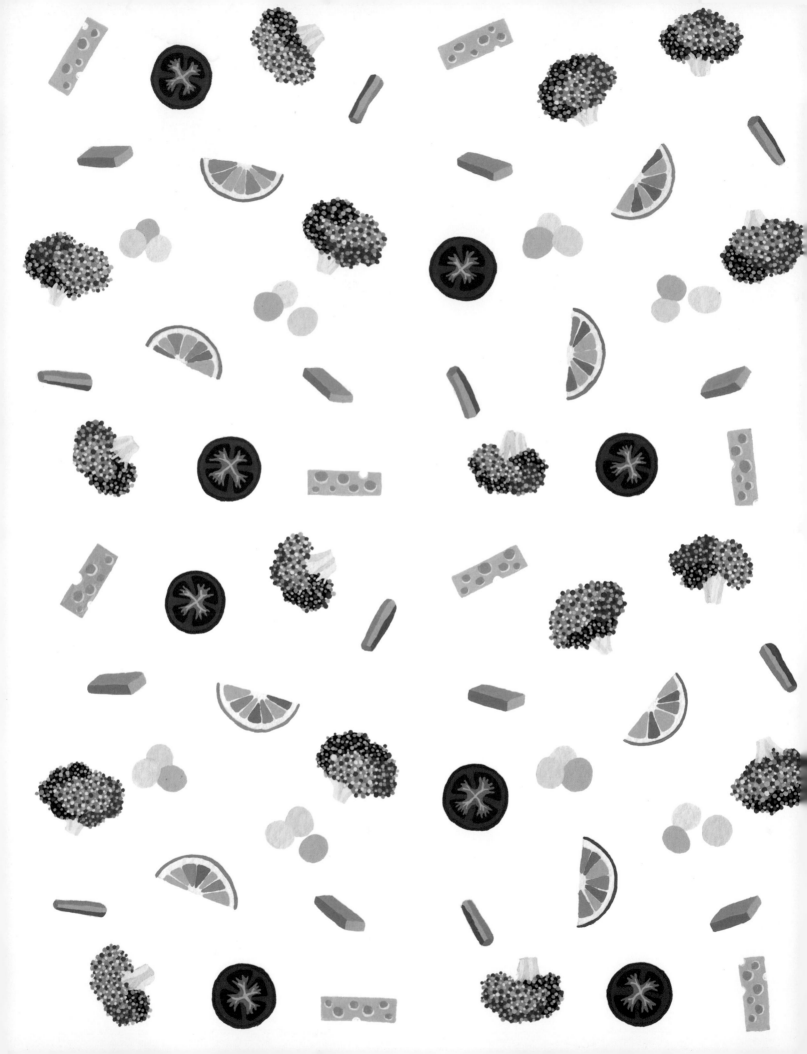

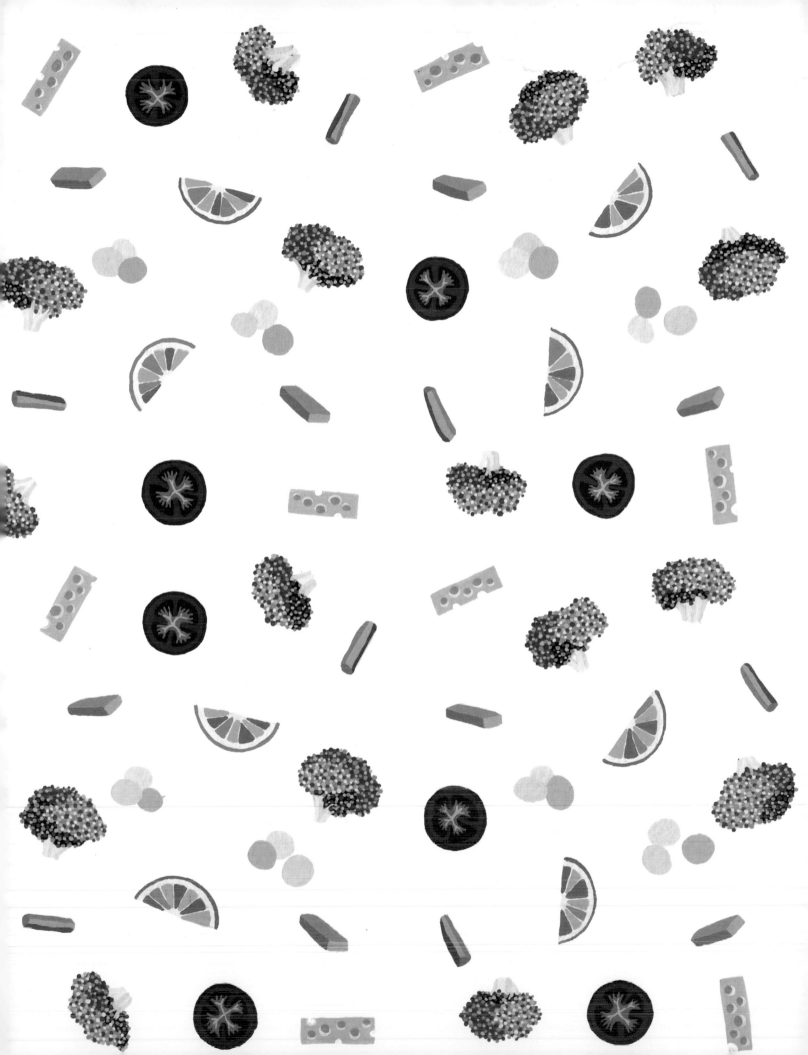